ESCAPE
from the
ISLAND

Written by Michael Butt

Illustrated by Philippe Dupasquier

◌ Collins

CHARACTERS

Narrator

Kim

Raffi

Pash

Ben

Alice

SCENE 1: IN THE BOAT

NARRATOR: Five friends are on holiday. One day, they go out in a small boat in the bay. The sea is calm. All of a sudden, Pash sees dark clouds heading towards them.

PASH: Look! It's a storm.

KIM: We'd better get back to shore!

RAFFI: It's coming too fast!

(sound effect: crash!)

NARRATOR: A big wave crashes into them. The boat flips over and throws everyone into the water.

PASH: Help!

BEN: We'll all drown!

ALICE: Hang on, everyone!

NARRATOR: The children are whirled through the water, but they hang on to the boat. The storm passes. The sea's calm again. But there's no sign of land.

(The friends scramble back aboard the boat.)

NARRATOR: Everyone's terrified; they can't see the shore any more. They're alone at sea.

BEN: I wish my dad was here.

RAFFI: Well, he's not.

ALICE: But we'll be OK.

BEN: How do you know?

NARRATOR: The sea is silent. It's like the world has turned to water.

KIM: The oars are still here. Who's the best rower?

PASH: Me, I expect.

RAFFI: You would say that.

ALICE: Stop it, both of you!

(Pash picks up the oars and tries to row.)

5

BEN: I'm hungry.

RAFFI: We're all hungry.

BEN: I'm really thirsty.

ALICE: Ben, be quiet.

BEN: I'm going to drink some seawater.

ALICE: Don't do that! It's salty. It'll make you thirstier.

BEN: *(sighing)* How will anyone find us?

NARRATOR: The friends feel very small. Suddenly …

KIM: *(pointing)* Look!

(Everyone looks out to sea.)

RAFFI: What is it?

BEN: *(nervously)* Is it another storm?

RAFFI: No. It's white. It's shining in the sun.

PASH: That's sand. Don't you see? It's an island!

ALICE: Come on, everybody. Row to the island!

SCENE 2: ON THE ISLAND

NARRATOR: They row until their hands turn red. They row until their shoulders ache. They row and they row until they land on the island.

(They drag the boat onto the beach.)

(Raffi runs towards a stream on the beach.)

RAFFI: Look! Fresh water.

(Everyone drinks thirstily, then flops down, tired out. A cool wind blows across the beach.)

BEN: *(shivering)* I'm cold.

PASH: We should build a shelter.

ALICE: She's right.

BEN: *(tearfully)* What? How long are we going to be here? I'm starving.

KIM: Ben's right too. We need food.

PASH: But I want to build a shelter. I know how to do it.

RAFFI: *(crossly)* You would!

ALICE: Why don't you and Ben find something to eat, Raffi? We'll stay here and build a shelter.

SCENE 3: IN THE UNDERGROWTH

(The girls are looking for leaves and branches.)

ALICE: Is this leaf big enough, Pash?

PASH: No, too small. It'll let the rain in.

KIM: What about this branch?

PASH: That'll do.

ALICE: How's it going to stand up?

PASH: You'll see. It'll look like a tent.

SCENE 4: ON THE SHORE

(Raffi and Ben are walking along the shore. Ben has picked up some purple fruit.)

BEN: Do you think we can eat these? They look like plums.

RAFFI: Nothing else has eaten them. They might be poisonous.

BEN: *(dropping the fruit)* But I'm starving! *(He kicks the sand.)* Ow!

RAFFI: What's the matter?

BEN: I just kicked something. Look, it's a piece of a mirror. *(He looks as if he might cry.)* Raffi, I want to go home.

RAFFI: We all do. But we need food. Come on, let's wash your foot in the sea, then try and catch some fish.

(Raffi and Ben return to the camp. Everyone's sitting on the sand looking miserable.)

RAFFI: Where's the shelter you were going to make?

PASH: The branches weren't strong enough.

KIM: It fell down.

BEN: *(nervously)* So, where will we go when it gets cold … and dark?

KIM: Well, where's the food *you* were going to get?

BEN: We couldn't catch any fish. I found this though. It's a broken mirror.

PASH: We can't eat a mirror, can we?

ALICE: Everybody, stop arguing! Let's get some sleep. We'll be OK.

SCENE 6: NIGHT-TIME

NARRATOR: The night comes down, dark and scary.

(Everyone huddles together on the beach.)

BEN: What's that noise?

ALICE: Go to sleep, Ben.

BEN: No, that whirring sound. Can't you hear it?

KIM: I can hear it. It's like a roaring.

RAFFI: It's coming from the other side of the hill.

ALICE: Let's go and see what it is.

RAFFI: You must be joking.

BEN: I'm not going.

KIM: Pash?

PASH: No, thank you!

ALICE: Listen!

NARRATOR: But the noise has stopped. Everyone sits quietly, listening, too hungry and scared to sleep.

SCENE 7: MORNING

NARRATOR: At last morning comes. The sun is already hot and the friends feel sticky and tired. They climb to the highest part of the island to see what was making the noise in the night. They look down – and can't believe their eyes.

ALICE and RAFFI: A helicopter!

KIM: It must have been looking for us!

(They all start to run down towards the helicopter.)

NARRATOR: The blades of the helicopter start up, whirring round and round.

PASH: It's taking off!

RAFFI: It's going to leave us!

ALICE: Stop! Stop!

KIM: Don't go!

BEN: Please don't go!

ALL: Don't leave us!

NARRATOR: But the pilot in the helicopter can't hear them. He's going to take off at any moment. Everyone shouts … everyone except Ben.

RAFFI: Ben, what are you doing?

PASH: *(crossly)* He's playing with his mirror. I can't believe it!

ALICE: Wait. I know what he's doing …

BEN: *(concentrating)* If I can get the sun to reflect off the mirror …

KIM: Yes! The pilot will see it!

(Ben points his mirror at the helicopter.)

NARRATOR: A small square of light shines in the pilot's eyes. The blades slow down as he stops the engine.

RAFFI: The pilot's seen us! He's getting out of the helicopter!

ALICE: We're saved! Ben, you're a star!

BEN: *(shyly)* Thank you.

PASH: That was good. But if I'd had that mirror, I'd have done it earlier …

RAFFI, ALICE, BEN and KIM: *(laughing)* Pash, will you be quiet!

SCENE 8: IN THE HELICOPTER

NARRATOR: Now the five friends are in the helicopter. It flies over their island. It looks beautiful, and they look down at the beach and the blue water. The palm trees wave their branches as though they're saying goodbye. The five friends wave to the island. They're going home.

The island

Ideas for guided reading

Learning objectives: give some reasons why things happen or characters change; explain their reactions to texts, commenting on important aspects; speak with clarity and use appropriate intonation when reading and reciting texts

Curriculum links: Art and design: People in action; Citizenship: Taking part – developing skills of communication and participation; Geography: An island home

Interest words: deserted, characters, narrator, terrified, nervously, thirstily, tearfully, crossly, shyly

Word count: 1,062

Resources: ICT, whiteboard, voice recorder

Getting started

- Look at the front cover with the children. Read the title together and notice that *Island* is spelt with a silent *s*.

- Invite the children to read the blurb aloud. Ask them to discuss with a partner how the friends might escape.

- Turn to p2. Read the characters' names and ask children to suggest what their personalities might be like, based on their pictures.

- Read the Narrator's first lines on p3. Discuss the role of the narrator in the play.

- Look at p3 with the children. Help children to decide which parts of the script are read aloud, and which parts provide extra information for the actors and director.

Reading and responding

- Help children to choose a character each. Ask them to skim through Scene 1 to find their character's lines and think about how they should be read, practising reading them aloud.

- Read Scene 1 together. Ask children to comment on each character's personality and what they think will happen next in the play.